Runaway Pony

Do you love ponies? Be a Pony Pal!

Look for these Pony Pal books:

PONY PALS

Runaway Pony

Jeanne Betancourt

illustrated by Paul Bachem

A
LITTLE APPLE
PAPERBACK

SCHOLASTIC INC.
New York Toronto London Auckland Sydney

No part of this publication may be reproduced in whole or in part, or stored in a retrieval system, or transmitted in any form or by any means, electronic, mechanical, photocopying, recording, or otherwise, without written permission of the publisher. For information regarding permission, write to Scholastic Inc., 555 Broadway, New York, NY 10012.

ISBN 0-590-54338-5

Text copyright © 1995 by Jeanne Betancourt.
Illustrations copyright © 1995 by Scholastic Inc.
All rights reserved. Published by Scholastic Inc.
APPLE PAPERBACKS and the APPLE PAPERBACKS logo are registered trademarks of Scholastic Inc.

12 11 10 9 8 7 6   8 9/9 0/0

Printed in the U.S.A.   40

First Scholastic printing, November 1995

The author thanks Dr. Kent Kay for medical consultation on this story.

A special thanks to Margaret Barney of Broken Wheel Ranch for western riding lessons.

Contents

Runaway Pony

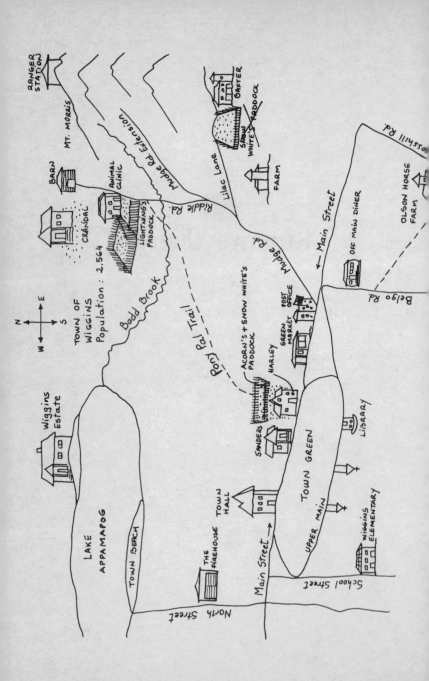

Strangles

Lulu leaned against the fence and watched her pony, Snow White, standing in the field. Snow White was sick. The beautiful pony had a stuffy nose, a bad cough, and a fever. Lulu wondered when her pony would be better.

Dr. Crandal had been treating Snow White for two weeks. He explained that Snow White had strangles, a contagious disease. Poor Snow White had to stay at the Baxters' stable where there were no other animals. Lulu felt badly that Snow White had to be separated from other ponies while she was sick. Lulu knew how much Snow White disliked being alone.

The sun was setting, and it was time to bring Snow White in for the night. "Come on, Snow White," Lulu called. "I cleaned out your stall. Let's go."

When Snow White saw Lulu coming toward her with a lead rope, she ran in the other direction. Lulu put the lead rope behind her back and held out an apple in her other hand. Snow White saw the apple and walked over to Lulu. As Snow White ate the apple, Lulu clipped the lead rope on the halter. "I'm sorry I tricked you," she said, "but it's for your own good."

Lulu led Snow White into the stable. While Lulu brushed Snow White, the pony looked through the open door to the field and whinnied. "You miss your pals, Acorn and Lightning," said Lulu. Snow White nudged Lulu on the shoulder. "I know how you feel. When I had strep throat, I couldn't see any of my friends, either."

Lulu added clean bedding to the stall,

piled hay in the hayrack, and put two hand-
fuls of oats in the feed bucket.

While Snow White ate, Lulu read the
Pony Care Chart. Dr. Crandal had visited
Snow White that day and written on the
chart. Lulu read his entry.

> FRIDAY, 10:00 AM
>
> LUNGS CLEARING.
> NO FEVER.
> LAST DOSE PENICILLIN.
> CAN GO HOME IN TWO DAYS.
>
> DR. C

"Snow White," Lulu shouted happily,
"you're coming home!" Lulu added her
entry to the Pony Care Chart.

> Friday, 5:30 P.M.
> 1/2 hour outdoors. More energy than
> yesterday.
> Did not want to come inside. Ate two
> handfuls of oats.
>
> Lulu

A horn honked. Lulu looked at her watch and knew it was Pam's mother. Mrs. Crandal was driving the Pony Pals to the movie theater in Milltown.

Lulu put on her backpack and said goodbye to Snow White. Snow White started to nicker and stomp around her stall. Snow White had never done that when Lulu was leaving her.

"I know you don't want to be alone, Snow White," Lulu said. "But you'll be coming home soon."

Snow White nickered again. Lulu wondered if she should stay with Snow White. But she really wanted to see the movie. The Pony Pals had talked about going all week. The horn honked again.

"I've got to go," Lulu told Snow White. Lulu kissed the pony on her soft cheek. "See you tomorrow," she said.

As Lulu ran across the frozen field to the car, she heard Snow White whinnying sadly. The pony seemed to be calling to Lulu, "Don't leave me."

Lulu opened the door to the Crandals' station wagon and climbed into the backseat with her friends.

"How's Snow White?" Pam and Anna asked at the same time.

"She's almost perfect again," Lulu said.

"My dad said she can come home on Sunday," said Pam.

"We're lucky the other ponies didn't catch it," Pam's mother said as she drove down Lilac Lane. "Strangles can be very serious."

"It's so great that Snow White is coming home," Anna said.

"Pretty soon we'll all be trail riding again," said Pam. "Just think, everything will be back to normal."

"I hope so," Lulu said. But all she could think about was Snow White's sad whinnies.

The Snowstorm

After the movie the Pony Pals and Mrs. Crandal went to Off-Main Diner. Anna's mother owned the diner and was working behind the counter.

Mrs. Crandal sat at the counter so that she and Mrs. Harley could talk. The girls went to their favorite booth in the back to write down what they wanted to eat. They were always their own waiter at the diner. While Lulu and Pam went behind the counter to pour their drinks, Anna went into the kitchen with their sandwich orders.

Lulu loved the way the Pony Pals worked together. Not just for simple things like getting their own food at the diner. But for big things, like solving difficult problems.

Pam and Lulu were waiting at the booth with their drinks when Anna came out of the kitchen with their sandwiches and fries. While the three friends ate, they made plans for the next day.

Anna offered to help Lulu with her morning chores for Snow White. For two weeks Lulu had been going to the Baxters' twice a day to take care of her pony. "After chores tomorrow, let's all go for a hike," suggested Anna.

"I'm training a pony for my mother's riding school at nine o'clock," Pam said. "But I can meet you at the Baxters' around ten-thirty."

"A hike sounds like fun," said Lulu. "But I'll be glad when we can all go trail riding together again." Pam and Anna agreed.

The Pony Pals loved to trail ride through the woods and fields around Wiggins. Snow

White and Anna's pony, Acorn, shared a paddock and shelter behind Anna's house. A mile-and-a-half trail, called Pony Pal Trail, connected that paddock to the Crandals' farm. Pam's pony, Lightning, lived there with many other Crandal ponies and horses.

Pam Crandal was a real horse lover and knew loads about them. She learned a lot from her dad, who was a veterinarian. Pam was a hard worker. She helped train ponies with her mom, who was a riding instructor. Pam was also the smartest person in their grade at school.

Anna Harley didn't like school very much. She was dyslexic, which meant reading and writing were hard for her. But Anna was smart, a great artist, and always full of fun.

Having good friends was especially important to Lulu. Her mother died when she was little and her dad often worked in faraway places. Anna and Pam had been friends since kindergarten. But Lulu didn't meet them until fifth grade when she moved to Wiggins to live with her grandmother.

Anna passed the plate of french fries to Lulu. "Let's have a welcome home party for Snow White," Anna said.

"We can make our ponies a special warm mash with oats, carrots, and apples," Pam said.

The Pony Pals hit high fives. A welcome home party for Snow White would be so much fun! Lulu was glad to have friends like her Pony Pals.

The next morning Lulu woke to see Wiggins covered with a thick blanket of snow. "I didn't know it was going to snow," she said to her grandmother at breakfast.

"The snow started around midnight," her grandmother said. "For a couple of hours it was blowing and coming down hard. The wind kept me awake. I'm surprised you slept through it."

There was a rap on the kitchen door and

Anna walked in. Her cheeks were red from the cold, but she was smiling. "I'm so glad we're going to be outside all day," she exclaimed.

"Me too," said Lulu.

"Brr-rr," said Grandmother Sanders. Lulu's grandmother wasn't the outdoor type. She owned a beauty parlor and cared more about looking proper than outdoor sports.

Lulu packed her backpack for the hike, put on her warmest jacket, and kissed her grandmother good-bye. Outside, the sky was blue and the wind had stopped blowing. Lulu and Anna tramped through the snow to the Baxters'.

"I love it when I'm the first one to walk in the snow," Anna said.

"Snow White does, too," said Lulu. "I can't wait to let her out in it."

The girls turned a corner in Lilac Lane and faced the Baxters' property. Lulu suddenly felt that something was wrong. As they walked closer she noticed that the paddock gate was open and blowing in the wind.

"I wonder who opened the door?" said Lulu.

"The stable door is open, too," said Anna.

The girls ran through the paddock to the stable. Snow White's stall was empty.

"Maybe she's outside and we didn't see her because she's white and the snow is white," Anna said.

Lulu and Anna ran back outside and looked all over the snowy paddock. All was quiet. They didn't see Snow White.

Lulu's pony was gone!

No Clues

"Oh, Anna," Lulu cried. "Where's Snow White?"

"Don't worry, Lulu," Anna said. "We'll find her."

"She wanted to go home with me last night," Lulu said. "Maybe that's where she went. Maybe she's in the paddock with Acorn right now."

Anna shook her head. "I would have seen her when I fed Acorn this morning," she said.

"And she wasn't on the road between our

house and here," said Lulu. "Or we would have seen her." Lulu felt like crying. But she knew tears wouldn't help find Snow White.

"When Snow White came down with strangles, we were at the Crandals'," said Lulu.

"And we came here right from there," added Anna, "so Snow White knows the way to the Crandals'."

"Maybe that's where she is," said Lulu.

Anna pointed toward Lilac Lane. "There's Pam. Let's ask her."

Anna and Lulu ran across the snowy field. The three friends met at the open gate.

"Did you see Snow White?" Anna and Lulu asked at the same time.

"No, isn't she here?" Pam asked. Her eyes were wide with surprise.

"Snow White ran away," said Anna.

"When?" asked Pam.

"She was gone when we got here," Anna answered.

"If Snow White didn't go home or to Pam's," Lulu said, "where did she go?"

"Let's look in the snow and see where her hoofprints lead," Pam suggested.

The girls looked all over the field. They didn't find one hoofprint.

"That's so strange," said Pam. "There are at least three inches of snow. How could Snow White run away and not make hoofprints?"

"Maybe she ran away while it was still snowing," said Anna. "Or maybe before it snowed."

"My grandmother told me it stopped snowing at about two in the morning," said Lulu.

"It's ten o'clock now," said Pam. "That means Snow White's been gone for at least eight hours already."

The Pony Pals looked at one another. They were all frightened for Snow White.

"Maybe she tried to go home or to Pam's," said Lulu, "and got lost because of the snowstorm." Lulu's eyes filled up with

17

tears. Pam put an arm around Lulu's shoulders. "Don't worry," she said, "we'll find Snow White."

"What if she hurt herself in the storm?" said Lulu. Her voice trembled. "What if she broke her leg?"

"Come on, Lulu," said Anna. "Let's see if Mrs. Baxter is home. Maybe she saw Snow White."

"And let's call the state police to see if anybody's reported seeing a lost pony," Pam suggested.

"Look," Anna said, "Mrs. Baxter is getting into her car."

As the girls ran toward the car they shouted to Mrs. Baxter to wait.

"Snow White's gone," Lulu said. "Did you see her anywhere?"

"No," said Mrs. Baxter. "What happened?"

"She ran away," answered Pam.

"Oh, dear," said Mrs. Baxter. "Poor Snow White. I have real estate appointments to show houses this morning, girls. But I'll come home right after. I want to help you find Snow White."

"Thank you," said Lulu. "Could we use your phone to call the state police?"

"Of course," answered Mrs. Baxter. "The kitchen door is unlocked. And the phone number for the police station is on the list of emergency numbers next to the phone. Stay there as long as you like."

The girls went into the house. Pam dialed the number for the state police and handed the phone to Lulu.

"I would like to report a missing pony," Lulu told the police officer who answered the phone.

The police officer asked Lulu a lot of questions like, "What color is the pony?" and "How big is the pony?" Then he said, "Hold on. I'll check the computer."

Lulu looked through the Baxters' kitchen window. She could see the open stable door and the empty paddock. Oh, Snow White, she thought. Where are you?

A minute later the officer was back on the phone with Lulu. "A dog was hit by a truck on Route Forty-one during the storm," he told her. "And there are two reports of cars hitting deer. Nothing about a pony. But it's early in the day," he added. "Something might still come in."

Lulu told the officer her grandmother's phone number and hung up the Baxters' phone.

Talking to the police gave Lulu a new idea of what might have happened to Snow White. "Maybe Snow White got hit by a car," she told her friends. "And she was injured or . . ." She couldn't finish the sentence.

"I wish ponies wore identification tags, like dogs," said Pam. "Then if someone found Snow White they'd know who to call."

"Snow White's so beautiful," said Lulu. "Maybe someone found her and wants to keep her."

"That would be better than being lost or hurt," said Anna.

"I don't think Snow White would like someone who would steal a pony," said Lulu.

"Don't worry, Lulu," Pam said. "We've solved big problems before. And we'll do it again."

"But we've always had clues to follow," said Lulu. She pointed out the window to the Baxters' snowy field. "Today the snow is covering up Snow White's tracks and any other clues she might have left."

"Lulu, you've tracked animals with your dad," Anna said.

"I was just thinking about that, too," said Pam. "You're great at tracking, Lulu."

Lulu wished her father was in Wiggins instead of in Africa. Mr. Sanders studied wild animals and wrote about them. Everything Lulu knew about tracking animals she had learned from her father.

Lulu couldn't help feeling happy for a

second. She loved it when the Pony Pals all had the same idea at the same time. But the happy feeling left quickly.

"If I had stayed with Snow White in the stable last night," Lulu said, "she wouldn't have run away. It's all my fault."

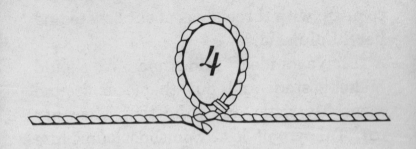

The Search Begins

The Pony Pals stayed in the Baxters' kitchen while they figured out what to do next.

Anna put her hand on Lulu's shoulder.

"Lulu, it was too cold for you to sleep in the stable last night," Anna said. "It's not your fault."

"I still should have stayed," said Lulu. "I have a warm sleeping bag."

"I know you feel badly, Lulu," Pam said. "But blaming yourself isn't going to find Snow White."

Lulu knew that Pam was right. "Let's come up with three ideas about how to find her," Lulu said.

"I have an idea," said Anna. "We should make posters and put them up around town. My sister and I did that when her cat, Tabby, got lost. Someone found him and called us because they saw the poster in the grocery store."

"Posters are a good idea," said Pam.

"Especially if Snow White got lost in town," said Lulu. "But if Snow White's lost in the woods, we have to find her ourselves."

"One of us could make posters for town," said Pam, "while the other two search the woods."

"Anna, you're the best artist," said Lulu. "Will you do the posters?"

"Sure," said Anna. She pulled a piece of paper from a message pad on the Baxters' kitchen counter. Anna went right to work on an idea for a missing pony poster.

"My idea is to search for Snow White on

Mudge Road Extension," said Lulu. She took a piece of paper from the pad, too. Then she drew a map.

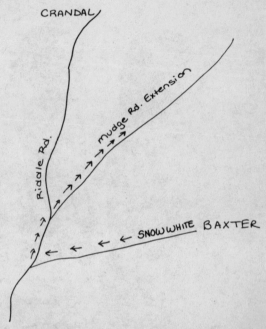

"I think Snow White was headed toward the Crandals'," explained Lulu. "Then the snowstorm started and she got lost. There aren't any roads going to the left, so Snow White probably went to the right." Lulu pointed to Mudge Road Extension. "We should look there."

"That's a good idea," said Pam.

"I wish I could make signs and search, too," said Anna.

"It's more important for you to make posters," said Lulu.

Anna showed her idea for a poster to Pam and Lulu. They helped her with spelling some of the words.

MISSING PONY

HER NAME IS SNOW WHITE

Color : white
Height : 13.2 hands (54 inches)
If found call : 555-0011

"That's perfect," said Lulu. "Making signs and putting them up is a big help, Anna."

"I'll go home and do them right away," Anna said.

While Anna was putting on her jacket, Pam told them her idea. "Lightning can help us find Snow White," she said. "Ponies have a great sense of smell."

"Aren't you afraid that she'll catch strangles?" asked Lulu.

"No," said Pam. "Finding Snow White is more important. If you were lost and had strep throat, we'd want to help find you. Even if we might catch it."

"Lightning and Acorn would feel the same way," added Anna.

"Thanks," said Lulu. "I think it's a good idea for Lightning to help. Besides, if Lightning finds Snow White, we can still keep them apart."

Anna opened the door to leave. "I'll come back here as soon as I'm finished with the signs," she told her friends. "Good luck."

After Anna left, Pam and Lulu made their plan. Pam would run home to tell her parents that Snow White was missing and to saddle up Lightning. Then Pam would ride Lightning to meet Lulu on Mudge Road. Meanwhile, Lulu would look for clues along Lilac Lane and Mudge Road. "But before I leave, I'll pack up emergency supplies and food for Snow White," Lulu said. "We'll need them . . . if we find her."

"We'll find her," Pam said. "Be sure to wait on Mudge Road for me, Lulu. Don't go into the woods alone. We have to stick together."

"I'll wait for you," promised Lulu.

Pam left the Baxters'.

Lulu already had water and an apple in her backpack. And her whistle was hanging around her neck. But there were other things she needed. Three clean dish towels were hanging on a rack. If Snow White had a bad cut, Lulu could use those towels for bandages. She knew Mrs. Baxter wouldn't mind if she borrowed them. So Lulu put them in her backpack. Next Lulu went out to the stable. She put a small bag of oats, a halter, and a lead rope in her backpack. She zipped the bag shut and ran out of the stable. She had to find her pony.

As she walked onto Lilac Lane, Lulu thought, I must have left Snow White's stall door open last night. That was how she broke out of the stable. And I didn't chain the paddock gate because I thought Snow White would be in the stable all night. I was in such a big hurry to go to the movie that I didn't take good care of my pony.

Lulu didn't bother to wipe away the tears that dropped on her cheek. She didn't care if they froze there. Her pony was lost.

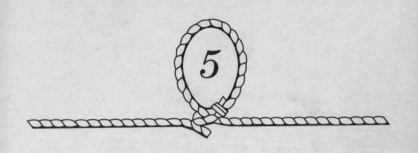

Lost

Lulu walked slowly along Lilac Lane. She was looking for clues that would lead her to Snow White. But she didn't see any. She turned right off Lilac Lane and headed up Mudge Road.

Lulu noticed some tracks in the snow along the edge of the road. As she ran toward the tracks she thought, Maybe Snow White didn't go off the road until the snow stopped. Maybe those are her tracks and I can follow them until I find her. Lulu ran up to the tracks and bent to study them.

They weren't tracks that a pony's hooves would make. Coyotes made those tracks. A whole pack of coyotes. What if Snow White was injured and coyotes found her? Lulu knew that coyotes killed injured or weak deer. Why not a pony?

Lulu was sad and worried as she walked on. But she was also determined to find her pony. She wished Pam and Lightning would hurry up.

Lulu was close to the spot where Mudge Road split into Riddle Road and Mudge Road Extension. She stared into the thick woods. Was Snow White somewhere in those woods? And if she was, why didn't she find her way out when it stopped snowing? Had Snow White fallen and hurt herself? Had the coyotes already found her?

Lulu remembered her father's advice about tracking animals. "Take your time and look for details. Most clues are small."

Lulu looked into the woods as she walked along. Suddenly she spotted a strand of creamy white hair caught on the low branch of a tree.

Was it hair from Snow White's mane? Lulu walked up to the tree. She knew the hair might be from a deer. She'd often seen the white hair from their tails caught on fences and branches. Lulu took off her gloves. She pulled the hair off the branch. The strands were much longer than the hair from a deer's tail. She rubbed the strands of hair between her fingers. They were coarse and oily like Snow White's mane. "Snow White," Lulu whispered toward the woods. "Snow White, you came this way."

Lulu had promised Pam she'd stay on the road. And Lulu's father had taught her never to go in the woods alone. But Lulu couldn't wait. She had to keep searching.

There were no trails to follow. And there was so much snow that she didn't know if she'd even recognize a trail if she found one. No wonder Snow White's lost, Lulu thought.

Lulu called out Snow White's name. Then she stood still and listened for an answer. All she heard was the soft plop of snow falling off pine tree limbs. She kept walking.

Lulu was discouraged. She had no idea how to find Snow White. And now she was lost. I could find my way back to Mudge Road by following my own tracks in the snow, she thought. But I'm not going back. Snow White came into the woods. She must be somewhere around here.

Lulu was thirsty. But she didn't drink the water in her backpack. I have to save it for Snow White, she thought. She looked up and saw that the sky was darkening with clouds. What if it snowed again? Snow would cover her tracks. How would Lulu find her way back to Mudge Road then?

As she walked farther into the woods, Lulu shouted out Snow White's name. But no familiar whinny answered her call. Once, through the trees, Lulu thought she saw Snow White lying down, covered with snow. Snow White is dead, she thought. Lulu pushed through the prickly brush to get to her pony. But the lump wasn't Snow White. It was a bush weighed down by snow.

Lulu saw a stone fence behind the bush. I'm on the Ridley farm, she thought. No one had lived on the Ridley farm for over one hundred and fifty years. The main house and barns had fallen down. All that was left were piles of stones and cellar holes where the buildings used to be. Some people said the Ridley farm was haunted. Lulu didn't believe in ghosts that much. But being alone on the Ridley farm still gave her the creeps.

Lulu walked on.

Soon she spotted a mound of manure in the snow. It looked as if it had come from a pony. Lulu broke off a branch from a tree and poked through the frozen outside layer of manure. Inside, the manure was still soft. Lulu's heart beat fast. Snow White left this pile, she thought. What other pony would be in these woods during a storm?

"Snow White!" Lulu called. "Can you hear me?" She called to her pony over and over again. In between her shouts, she listened for a response.

Finally Lulu heard something. She listened carefully. It was Snow White's whinny!

"I'm coming, Snow White!" Lulu shouted. Snow White whinnied again. This time Lulu paid attention to the direction Snow White's call came from. She turned to her right and ran toward the sound.

Lulu's heart was pounding. She was excited and frightened. She found Snow White. But her pony's whinny sounded hoarse. Was Snow White's strangles worse? Was she injured? And how would Lulu get Snow White out of the woods?

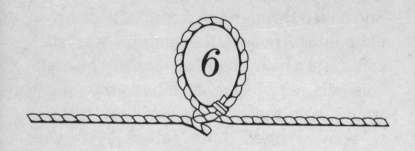

S.O.S.

Lulu ran through the cold and snowy woods toward the sound of her pony's whinny. "I'm coming!" Lulu shouted. She pushed through the bush into a clearing.

Snow White's call sounded very close now. Lulu stopped and looked around. She could hear Snow White, but she could not see her. Was that because her pony was the color of snow? Or was Snow White buried *under* snow?

Finally, Lulu realized that Snow White's whinny was coming from in the ground.

Lulu came to the edge of a hole that had been the cellar for the Ridley farmhouse. She looked down and saw . . . Snow White!

Snow White looked up and saw Lulu, too. The pony nickered happily and charged around the floor of the cellar. Lulu realized that Snow White had jumped or fallen into the hole and couldn't get out. She was relieved to see that Snow White hadn't broken any bones. The pony nickered again. She seemed to be saying, "Glad to see you, Lulu. Now get me out of here."

Lulu lay on her stomach and reached out her arm. Snow White came over to her. "Snow White," she said. "I'm so glad you're all right and that I found you." Lulu stroked Snow White's forehead. Snow White's hide felt warm. Did she have a fever again? Was her strangles worse? Lulu had to work quickly.

Snow White probably hadn't had food or water since the evening before. Lulu took her water bottle and the bag of oats out of her backpack. Lulu wondered if she should

jump into the cellar hole to be with Snow White. The sides of the cellar were crumbling stone walls covered with ice and snow. If I go down there, Lulu thought, I might not be able to get out.

Lulu decided to stay where she was and leaned carefully over the cellar hole. Snow White lapped water out of Lulu's hand and ate the oats and an apple. When Snow White was finished eating, she looked up at Lulu and whinnied. Lulu knew her pony was saying, "That was good. Now get me out of here."

"Don't worry, Snow White," Lulu said. "I'll get you out." Lulu wished with all her heart that her Pony Pals were with her. She needed Pony Pal Power. Maybe Pam and Lightning were in the woods now. Lulu was about to shout out Pam's name when she remembered her whistle.

Lulu's father gave the Pony Pals whistles when they went on their first overnight camping trip. The Pony Pals all used the same signals. Their S.O.S. signal was one short blast, one long blast, and another short one. The response was one long blast and that meant someone was on the way to help. Lulu raised the red plastic whistle to her lips and blew out the S.O.S. signal. Snow White was startled by the loud noise. She charged nervously around her ice-and-snow prison.

Lulu leaned over the hole again. "Sorry, Snow White," she said. She showed Snow White the whistle and blew again. This time Lulu blew softly, so Snow White could get used to the sound. The next time she blew loudly. By then Snow White wasn't afraid of the noise anymore.

After each S.O.S. call, Lulu listened for a whistle in response. Usually Lulu loved the silence of Wiggins woods, but not today. Maybe Pam doesn't have her whistle with her like I do, thought Lulu. Or maybe she's too far away to hear mine.

Lulu squatted down at the edge of the hole to pat her pony on the head. "Don't worry, Snow White," she said. "We'll get you help." Snow White threw back her head and nickered.

Lulu smiled at her pony. She stood up to try the whistle signal once more. As she stood, Lulu lost her balance and tumbled into the eight-foot-deep hole.

Lulu scrambled to her feet. Snow White gave Lulu a nudge on the shoulder. Lulu hugged her pony. "I'm okay, Snow White," she said. "But I think we're in deep trouble now."

Lulu looked around the cellar hole. One side wasn't as steep as the other three. But it was still too steep and icy for her to climb. Snow White and Lulu were both prisoners in the freezing hole.

"What a mess we're in," Lulu said. "And it's all my fault. I didn't lock the stall door or the gate and you ran away. None of this would have happened if I'd slept in the stable last night. I'm sorry, Snow White."

Snow White nudged Lulu again. The pony knew Lulu was upset and wanted her to feel better.

"Snow White, you deserve a better owner than me," said Lulu. "Someone who isn't selfish and doesn't think a silly movie is more important than her sick pony."

Being with Snow White made Lulu feel brave again. She had to get help for her pony. She knew the sound of her whistle wouldn't be loud enough coming out of the cellar hole. Lulu needed to be higher up. And the only way to do that was to get on Snow White's back.

"Snow White," she said, "I didn't have on my backpack when I fell. So I don't have your halter and lead rope. But if I could sit on you, I'd be higher up. Then maybe Pam will hear our S.O.S."

Lulu had sat on Snow White's bare back before. But she had always had a halter and rope to hold onto. She moved Snow White over to a rock. Lulu placed her left foot on the rock and flung her right leg over her pony's side. Snow White stayed perfectly still. Lulu leaned forward, stroked Snow

White's neck, and whispered, "You're the most wonderful pony in the world."

Lulu held onto Snow White's mane with one hand and raised the whistle to her lips with the other. She blew out her S.O.S. signal and wished that someone would hear her call.

The sky was full of storm clouds. Lulu watched the gray clouds gather. She shivered. It was getting colder and darker. Lulu wondered what would happen to her and Snow White if they were in the snowy prison overnight. Would her pony survive? Would she?

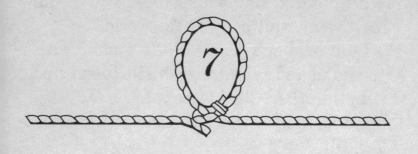

The Ice Prison

Lulu sat on Snow White's back and blew S.O.S. signals with her whistle. Suddenly, Snow White whinnied and pawed the ground. Lulu jumped off Snow White's back. As her feet hit the ground she heard a pony answer Snow White's call. She also heard Pam yelling, "Lulu, Lulu, where are you?"

"In here!" Lulu shouted back. "In a cellar hole!"

A minute later Pam and Lightning were

looking over the edge of the hole. "Lulu, are you all right?" Pam asked.

"I'm okay," answered Lulu. "But I think Snow White's strangles is worse."

"How did she get down there?" asked Pam.

"I don't know," answered Lulu. "I guess she fell in, like I did."

Pam tied Lightning's lead rope to a tree. Then she leaned over the edge of the cellar hole and put out her hand. "If you hold on to me," she said, "maybe you can climb out."

Lulu put her hands behind her back and shook her head no. "I'll stay with Snow White," she said. "If I leave she might try to follow me. She could break a leg."

"Why didn't you wait for me on the road?" Pam asked.

"Why'd you take so long?" said Lulu.

"I was looking for my parents to help us," Pam said. "My mother had gone someplace with my sister and brother. And my father is operating on a horse. I couldn't interrupt him. But I left him a note to telephone us when he finished."

"Telephone us?" exclaimed Lulu. "Here? In the woods?"

Pam patted her jacket pocket. "I borrowed his cellular phone," she said. "I don't think he'll mind. This is an emergency."

"Pam!" a girl's voice shouted. It was followed by a pony's whinny. Lulu recognized both the voice and the whinny. It was Anna and Acorn!

"Where's Lulu?" Anna asked Pam.

"Anna, I'm down here!" shouted Lulu.

Anna rode Acorn up to the edge of the hole and looked down. "You found Snow White!" she exclaimed. "Oh, Snow White, we were so worried about you."

"I'm glad you're here to help us get her out," said Lulu.

"Anna, how'd you get here so fast?" asked Pam.

"I only made one missing poster," said Anna as she dismounted Acorn. "My sis-

ter's making copies and putting signs up around town. But we don't need missing pony posters anymore. You found Snow White."

"But how did you find us?" asked Lulu.

"I followed the tracks in the snow," said Anna.

"We have to get Snow White out of here," said Lulu. "She's tired. And I think she has a fever again."

"My dad said to keep Snow White warm while she has strangles," said Pam. "It's bad for her to be out in the cold for so long."

Acorn moved closer to the edge of the cellar hole and looked at Snow White. Snow White looked back at Acorn. Anna grabbed Acorn's lead rope to keep him from going any closer to the edge.

"Anna, you'd better tie Acorn to the tree with Lightning," said Pam.

When Acorn was safely tied, the three girls talked about the problem of getting Snow White out of the hole. Pam showed

Anna the telephone. "That was a great idea," said Anna. "But I wish your dad would hurry up and call us. We could really use his help."

"Well, for now, it's up to us," said Pam. "We've got to come up with a plan. Every minute that Snow White is out here is bad for her."

"Maybe a snowmobile could drag Snow White out," said Anna. "All we'd need is some rope, a big blanket, and the snowmobile."

"But we'd have to tranquilize Snow White first," said Pam. "Then she'd be too sleepy to walk back. And we can't drag her through the woods."

"But the snowmobile part of your idea is great, Anna," said Lulu. "What if a snowmobile brought in some salt and sand. We could spread it on the wall to melt the ice. Then with the halter and lead rope, we could help Snow White climb out."

"We have loads of sand and salt at my

place," said Pam. "And my dad could get our neighbor Mr. Trono to drive it in with his snowmobile."

Lulu pointed at the slanted wall that wasn't as steep as the others. "If we salt and sand that wall," she said, "I bet Snow White could climb out."

Just then Lightning and Acorn snorted and whinnied in Snow White's direction.

Snow White pawed the ground and looked up as she called back to her friends.

"I'm afraid she'll try to climb out now," said Lulu. "I have a halter and lead rope in my backpack. Throw them down to me so I can hold on to her."

Lightning and Acorn snorted again. And Snow White answered. She sounded very upset.

Anna dropped the halter and lead rope into the cellar hole. But before Lulu could pick them up, Snow White began charging around the hole. Lulu couldn't bend down to get the halter and lead rope while Snow White was moving around. She had to stay clear of her pony's hooves. "Careful, Lulu," Pam warned.

Lightning and Acorn kept up their whinnies and snorts.

Snow White stomped and snorted back.

"Snow White!" Lulu yelled. "Stop. Please, stop!"

But Snow White didn't hear Lulu. She was listening to her pony friends. And she wanted to be with them. Snow White turned toward the slanted wall. She backed up. Then she snorted one more time and ran toward it.

"Oh, no!" Anna shouted. "She's going to try to climb out."

"Lulu, grab her mane!" Pam yelled.

But it was too late. Snow White was already climbing up the wall.

The wall was very steep and slippery. Snow White could easily fall and break a leg. The Pony Pals watched and held their breath.

You Can Do It!

Snow White was slipping backwards on the ice-covered rock wall. If Snow White couldn't make it out of the hole, she would crash to the cellar floor. Lulu knew only one thing the Pony Pals could do to help her. They had to cheer her on.

"You can do it, Snow White!" Lulu shouted. "I know you can."

Lightning and Acorn encouraged Snow White with loud whinnies.

"Come on, Snow White!" yelled Pam. "You're almost there."

"Go for it, Snow White!" screamed Anna.

Snow White scrambled to the top and climbed out herself. Pam and Anna cheered for her. But Snow White ignored them and ran over to her pony friends.

"Is Snow White okay?" Lulu shouted to Pam and Anna.

"There's one little cut on her shoulder," said Pam. "But it's nothing to worry about."

"Better keep her from the others," said Lulu, "because of the strangles."

But Snow White was already leaving the other ponies. She walked back over to the hole and whinnied at Lulu as if to say, "What are you still doing down there? Come on up."

"Grab her," Lulu shouted. "Before she falls back in!"

"I can't," said Pam. "She doesn't have on a halter."

"I've got pony treats in my pockets," said Anna. "I'll distract her."

Meanwhile, Lulu picked up Snow White's halter and lead rope. She tied them in a big knot and threw them up to Pam. It took three tries, but finally they landed over the top. Pam handed the halter and lead rope to Anna.

"I better get out of here myself," Lulu told Pam.

Pam lay on the snow and dropped her arm toward Lulu. But their hands didn't touch. The hole was too deep. "Wait a minute," said Pam. "I have an extra lead rope in my saddlebag."

Lulu looked up at the slippery wall Snow White had just climbed. She saw drops of blood left by Snow White's cut. Lulu thought, I'll have to be as brave as my pony.

Pam stretched out in the snow again and dropped one end of the rope to Lulu. Lulu dug her foot into the snowy rock ledge and began to take one slippery step after another.

Snow White nickered to Lulu as if to say, "Come on, you can do it."

When Lulu reached the top, she hugged her pony. They were both safe.

But Lulu was happy for only a second. Snow White felt warm against her cheek and she was panting. Was Snow White's strangles worse?

A ringing sound startled the girls and their ponies. "What's that?" Anna said.

Pam giggled. "It's the telephone," she said.

Pam took the phone out of her pocket and talked into it. "Hi, Dad," she said. Pam told her father all about the cellar hole prison; how Snow White climbed out to be with Lightning and Acorn; and how Lulu had climbed out using a lead rope.

"Let me talk to him," said Lulu. She told Dr. Crandal that Snow White was feverish and shivering.

"Bring her right into the clinic," Dr. Crandal said. "I'll check her out."

"I'm afraid Lightning and Acorn will catch strangles from Snow White," said Lulu.

"Keep them apart as best you can," he said.

Lulu said good-bye to Dr. Crandal and handed the phone back to Pam. Lulu patted Snow White on the cheek. "Sorry," she said, "you still can't be with your friends." Then she told Pam and Anna, "We have to take Snow White to the clinic."

The three girls led their ponies single file through the silent, snowy woods. Lulu and Snow White went first. After they'd gone a little way, Lulu shouted back to Pam and Anna, "You guys have saddles. You can ride home. I'll lead Snow White out following your tracks."

"I'll walk with you," said Anna.

"Me too," said Pam. "We should stick together."

As the Pony Pals walked along, Lulu could hear Pam and Anna talking about their adventure. But Lulu was quiet. She was still worried about Snow White.

When they reached the Crandals', Pam and Anna took their ponies to the barn. But Lulu went straight to the clinic with Snow White. Dr. Crandal met her at the door.

"Well, Snow White," he said, "I hear you've had quite an experience. Let's take a look at you."

Dr. Crandal smiled at Lulu and patted her on the shoulder. "You look a little worn out yourself, Lulu."

"I'm okay," said Lulu.

Dr. Crandal led Snow White into the examination room and cross-tied her. Lulu watched as he took Snow White's temperature, looked into her throat and nose, and felt her glands.

Dr. Crandal was finishing up his exam when Pam and Anna came into the room. "How is she, Dad?" asked Pam.

"She's doing all right," said Dr. Crandal. He smiled at Lulu. "Strangles isn't a problem anymore. She's just cold and tired. Since you have an open shelter at home, Lulu, it would be better if you left Snow White here overnight. A blanket, a warm mash, and a good night's sleep inside will do wonders for her."

"Can Lulu ride Snow White tomorrow?" asked Anna.

"Sure," answered Dr. Crandal. "But I'd take it easy the first time she's out. It will be a few days before she's one hundred percent again." Dr. Crandal went back into his office to meet his next patient.

"*All right!*" said Pam. "We found Snow White. And she's going to be okay."

"And we can all go trail riding together again," said Anna.

Pam and Anna raised right hands to hit high fives. But Lulu didn't raise her hand. She ran outside. She didn't want her friends to see that she was crying. Lulu knew that everything was not okay. She'd left Snow White alone and hadn't locked her stall door. She'd left the paddock gate unlocked, too. She'd almost killed her pony.

A Letter

Pam and Anna ran out to find Lulu. She was sitting on the paddock fence, crying.

"What's wrong, Lulu?" Anna asked.

"You don't understand," Lulu whispered. "It was all my fault."

"It's not your fault, Lulu," Pam said.

But Lulu just kept crying.

"I have an idea," said Pam. "Snow White's sleeping over and Acorn's already here. Let's have a Pony Pal barn sleepover tonight. There's even a heater in my mother's office."

"Then tomorrow we can go trail riding from here," said Anna.

"I can't sleep over," said Lulu. "My grandmother wants me to stay home tonight."

"When you tell her everything that's happened, I bet she'll let you sleep over," said Anna.

Lulu shook her head. "I want to go home."

Lulu saw Pam and Anna look at each other. But they didn't say any more about a sleepover.

After Lulu put Snow White in a stall in the barn, the Pony Pals went into Mrs. Crandal's office. Anna phoned her sister to tell her they'd found Snow White. Pam called Mrs. Baxter with the same good news. Meanwhile, Lulu made a warm mash for Snow White.

RECIPE FOR WARM MASH
Ingredients:

    2 handfuls of oats
    ½ quart bran
    2 cut-up apples
    2 cut-up carrots

Directions:

    Mix all ingredients.
    Add hot tap water.
    Stir well.

Anna helped Lulu make the mash. "I'll go home when you do," said Anna. "Acorn and I will walk with you. It'll be pretty on Pony Pal Trail with all the snow."

"I'm going to ask my grandmother to pick me up," said Lulu. "I'm pretty tired."

"You can ride Acorn and I'll walk," said Anna.

"My grandmother will pick me up," said Lulu. She left the office with the bowl of warm mash for Snow White.

Lulu fed Snow White and made sure her blanket was on snugly. Then she gave her pony a hug. "I love you Snow White," she said. "I'm really sorry."

Lulu stayed with Snow White until her grandmother came to pick her up. Anna and Pam followed Lulu to the car. Lulu climbed into the car beside her grandmother.

"See you tomorrow," called Pam.

"Don't forget about trail riding," added Anna.

"Bye," said Lulu.

Grandmother Sanders didn't like horses very much. But she knew Lulu did. "Tell me exactly what happened today," she said. Lulu told her everything except the scariest parts. When Lulu finished her story, Grandmother Sanders sighed. "Lucinda, you are so much like your mother. She was crazy about the outdoors and animals just like you."

Lulu's father told Lulu many stories about her mother. Her mother loved horses, too. But my mother took good care of her

horses, Lulu thought. A careless person like me doesn't deserve to have a pony.

By the time Lulu was ready for bed, she knew what she had to do. She sat at her desk, turned on the lamp, and took her stationery and a pen out of the drawer. She was ready to write a letter.

Dear Mrs. Crandal:

I want to give Snow White to you. You can use her in your riding school.

Snow White and Lightning are good friends. I know that Snow White will be very happy living at your place. I also know that you take very good care of your horses. So she will be safe, too.

Please let me know if you will take Snow White.

Sincerely yours,
Lulu Sanders

Lulu folded the letter and put it in an envelope. Then she went to bed and cried herself to sleep.

The next morning Lulu woke up to a knock on her bedroom door. "Lucinda," Grandmother Sanders called through the door. "Anna telephoned to say it's time to go trail riding."

Lulu opened her eyes and looked at her bedside clock. It was nine o'clock. She put on her bathrobe and went down to the kitchen. Anna was knocking on the door. Lulu let her in.

"You sleepyhead!" Anna teased. "I've been up for hours. I think Acorn knows we're all going trail riding together. He's so excited. Hurry up. Get dressed."

"I'm not going with you," said Lulu. "I think Snow White should rest for another day."

"But Dr. Crandal said — "

"Besides I don't feel like riding today," added Lulu.

"But you love to trail ride," said Anna.

"I don't want to go and I don't want to talk about it," said Lulu.

Anna frowned. "If that's the way you want to be," she said.

Lulu reached into her bathrobe pocket and took out a sealed envelope. "Can you give this to Mrs. Crandal for me?" she said.

Anna took the envelope and looked at it. "What is it?" she asked.

"Just a letter," snapped Lulu.

Lulu couldn't explain. No one would understand. Not even her Pony Pals.

The Velvet Skirt

After Anna left, Lulu sat at the kitchen table and stared out into the yard. Grandmother was surprised to find her sitting there. "Aren't you riding with your friends today?" she asked.

Lulu shook her head no.

"Are you going hiking?" asked Grandmother Sanders.

"I'm going to stay indoors today," said Lulu.

"Goodness gracious," said Grandmother. "Now that's a surprise. Well, I'm going to an *indoor* brunch and an *indoor* concert with Mrs. Addison. Would you like to join us?"

"Okay," said Lulu.

A little later Grandmother met Lulu in the upstairs hall. "While you were in the shower, Pam telephoned," she said.

"Is Snow White okay?" asked Lulu.

"Pam said she's good as new. And she wanted to know what time you were coming over to go trail riding."

"Did you tell her I wasn't going?" asked Lulu.

"I told her you were going to brunch and a concert with me," answered Grandmother.

"Good," said Lulu.

Grandmother smiled. "Lucinda, dear," she said, "wear that lovely velvet skirt and the sweater with the lace collar that I bought you. You look so lovely in that outfit."

Lulu didn't care what she did or what she wore. So she put on the outfit. She even let

Grandmother fix her hair with a big lacy ribbon.

Off-Main Diner was always crowded for Sunday brunch. But Mrs. Harley made sure there was a table for her neighbors. She led them to the Pony Pals' favorite booth in the back of the diner.

"Lulu, I thought you were riding with Anna and Pam today," said Mrs. Harley.

"I'm resting today," Lulu told her.

During brunch Lulu only half-listened to Mrs. Addison and Grandmother's conversation. And she only half-ate her French toast. Her mind was on Snow White. She wondered if Snow White would miss her. Maybe she'll miss me a little bit at first, thought Lulu. But she'll be with Lightning and familiar people. And she'll be safe.

Grandmother, Mrs. Addison, and Lulu were ready to leave when Pam and Anna came running into the diner. They ran right over to the booth.

"I thought you guys were going trail riding today," said Lulu.

"We have a Pony Pal Problem to solve today," said Anna.

"We've already had one meeting," added Pam.

Lulu knew that she was the Pony Pal Problem and that the meeting had been about her. She wondered if her friends understood that she wasn't going to be a Pony Pal anymore. That she didn't deserve to be a Pony Pal.

"We're having another meeting now," said Anna. "And you have to stay for it."

"I'm going to a concert," said Lulu.

"Lulu Sanders, this is the most important meeting we've ever had," said Pam.

"Can't we have the meeting after school tomorrow?" said Lulu.

"*No!*" said Pam and Anna in unison. They said it so loudly that everyone in the diner looked at them.

"Lucinda, I think you should stay for the meeting," said Grandmother. "You haven't been yourself today. Maybe your friends can help you out of your bad mood."

After Grandmother Sanders and Mrs. Addison left, the Pony Pals settled down for their meeting.

"Do you know what our meeting was about this morning?" asked Pam.

"About my giving Snow White away to your mother," said Lulu.

"Why do you want to give Snow White away?" asked Anna.

"Anna, you know why," said Lulu. "Snow White wouldn't have been lost if it weren't for me. It was all my fault. I don't deserve to have a pony. I've made up my mind and nothing you say is going to change it."

Lulu stood up to go. "If Pam's mother won't take Snow White," she said, "I'll ask Mr. Olson to sell her through his horse farm."

Anna grabbed Lulu's skirt. "You can't go," she said. "You have to stay and hear our ideas about this problem."

"Let go of me," said Lulu. She pulled to get away from Anna. But Anna held on tight. The Pony Pals all heard the ripping sound the skirt made as it tore away from the waist.

"You better sit down," said Pam. "Before your skirt comes all the way off."

11

2 Ideas + 1

Lulu sat back down.

Pam handed her a slip of paper. "Read my solution to our Lulu problem," said Pam. "Read it out loud."

"Read it yourself," said Lulu angrily.

Lulu, it's not your fault that Snow White got out. You didn't leave the door open. Snow White broke the lock.

"How do you know the lock broke?" asked Lulu. "You just made that up."

"I did not," said Pam. "I wouldn't lie."

"Pam and I were just over there and looked at it ourselves," said Anna. "We saw that the lock was ripped right out of the wood."

"We can show you if you still don't believe us," said Pam. "Mrs. Baxter said the wood must have been rotten. She feels awful about it."

"And even if you did leave the stall door unlocked," said Anna, "that's no reason to give up Snow White. Everybody makes mistakes."

"But I knew she was lonely that night and I didn't stay with her," said Lulu sadly.

"So what?" said Pam. "Everybody gets lonely sometimes. Even ponies. You're making a big deal out of nothing. My mother thinks so, too."

"Now look at my idea," said Anna.

FRIENDS 4-EVER

Lulu looked at the drawing. She wasn't angry anymore. Her friends were right. She shouldn't give up Snow White. But she didn't let Pam and Anna know she agreed with them yet.

"Something is still wrong," Lulu said.

"What?" asked Pam and Anna.

"Whenever we solve problems we come up with three ideas, not two. So I have to have an idea. It's my turn." Lulu turned Pam's paper over and wrote on it. Then she put the paper in the middle of the table. The Pony Pals read Lulu's idea out loud.

"I'm sorry I didn't wait for Pam before we searched for Snow White," said Lulu. "I shouldn't have gone alone."

"If my pony had run away," said Pam, "I might have done the same thing."

"Me, too," said Anna.

"But we all have to remember that we work best when we work together," said Pam.

"Lulu, you had us really scared," said Anna. "I was so afraid you wouldn't understand. You can be very stubborn."

"I didn't feel like a Pony Pal anymore," said Lulu. "It's an awful feeling."

"You don't look like one either with that bow in your hair," said Anna with a giggle.

"And that fancy outfit," added Pam.

Lulu glanced at her own reflection in the diner window and laughed. "I see what you mean," she said.

"There's still time for our trail ride," said Pam. "Come on. Let's go."

"I can't leave this booth," said Lulu. "My skirt's ripped."

Anna got safety pins from the kitchen and pinned Lulu's skirt back together. Then the Pony Pals put on their jackets and left the diner.

When Lulu came out the front door she saw that their three ponies were tied to the diner's hitching post.

"Snow White!" Lulu shouted. "How did you get here?"

Snow White looked up and whinnied happily at Lulu.

"We rode over and ponied Snow White behind us on the lead rope," said Pam.

Lulu ran to Snow White and gave her a big hug. "How could I even have thought of giving you away?" she said.

"We better go over to your place so you can change," said Pam. "You can't ride in a skirt."

"Oh, yes I can," said Lulu. "My shoes have heels. And I bet you brought my helmet."

Pam laughed as she opened her backpack. She pulled out Lulu's helmet and handed it to her.

The three girls put on their helmets and untied their ponies from the hitching post.

Lulu placed her left foot in the stirrup and swung up on Snow White. *"All right!"* she shouted. The Pony Pals moved their ponies close together and hit high fives.

The ponies whinnied happily. Lulu turned Snow White toward the road. She knew she looked strange horseback riding in a skirt and her best shoes. But she didn't care. She was riding Snow White again.

Dear Reader:

I am having a lot of fun researching and writing books about the Pony Pals. I've met many interesting kids and adults who love ponies. And I've visited some wonderful ponies at homes, farms, and riding schools.

Before writing Pony Pals I wrote fourteen novels for children and young adults. Four of these were honored by Children's Choice Awards.

I live in Sharon, Connecticut, with my husband, Lee, and our dog, Willie. Our daughter is all grown up and has her own apartment in New York City.

Besides writing novels I like to draw, paint, garden, and swim. I didn't have a pony when I was growing up, but I have always loved them and dreamt about riding. Now I take riding lessons on a horse named Saz.

I like reading and writing about ponies as much as I do riding. Which proves to me that you don't have to ride a pony to love them. And you certainly don't need a pony to be a Pony Pal.

Happy Reading,

Jeanne Betancourt

Be a Pony Pal®!

**Anna, Pam, and Lulu want you to join them
on adventures with their favorite ponies!**

**Order now and you get a free pony portrait bookmark and two
collecting cards in all the books—for you _and_ your pony pal!**

❑ BBC48583-0	#1 I Want a Pony	$2.99
❑ BBC48584-9	#2 A Pony for Keeps	$2.99
❑ BBC48585-7	#3 A Pony in Trouble	$2.99
❑ BBC48586-5	#4 Give Me Back My Pony	$2.99
❑ BBC25244-5	#5 Pony to the Rescue	$2.99
❑ BBC25245-3	#6 Too Many Ponies	$2.99
❑ BBC54338-5	#7 Runaway Pony	$2.99
❑ BBC54339-3	#8 Good-bye Pony	$2.99
❑ BBC62974-3	#9 The Wild Pony	$2.99
❑ BBC62975-1	#10 Don't Hurt My Pony	$2.99
❑ BBC86597-8	#11 Circus Pony	$2.99
❑ BBC86598-6	#12 Keep Out, Pony!	$2.99
❑ BBC86600-1	#13 The Girl Who Hated Ponies	$2.99
❑ BBC86601-X	#14 Pony-Sitters	$3.50
❑ BBC86632-X	#15 The Blind Pony	$3.50
❑ BBC74210-8	Pony Pals Super Special #1:The Baby Pony	$5.99

Available wherever you buy books, or use this order form.

....

Send orders to Scholastic Inc., P.O. Box 7500, 2931 East McCarty Street, Jefferson City, MO 65102

Please send me the books I have checked above. I am enclosing $_____ (please add $2.00 to cover shipping and handling). Send check or money order — no cash or C.O.D.s please.

Please allow four to six weeks for delivery. Offer good in the U.S.A. only. Sorry, mail orders are not available to residents in Canada. Prices subject to change.

Name_____ Birthdate ___/___/___

    First   Last   M   D   Y

Address_____

City_____ State_____ Zip_____

Telephone (   ) _____ ❑ Boy   ❑ Girl

Where did you buy this book?   ❑ Bookstore   ❑ Book Fair   ❑ Book Club   ❑ Other